Sarah Orne Jewett

Betty Leicester's Christmas

Sarah Orne Jewett

Betty Leicester's Christmas

ISBN/EAN: 9783741194412

Manufactured in Europe, USA, Canada, Australia, Japa

Cover: Foto ©Andreas Hilbeck / pixelio.de

Manufactured and distributed by brebook publishing software
(www.brebook.com)

Sarah Orne Jewett

Betty Leicester's Christmas

IN SOLEMN MAJESTY (page 62)

BETTY LEICESTER'S
CHRISTMAS

BY

SARAH ORNE JEWETT

BOSTON AND NEW YORK
HOUGHTON, MIFFLIN AND COMPANY
The Riverside Press, Cambridge
1899

To
M. E. G.

LIST OF ILLUSTRATIONS

BETTY LEICESTER'S CHRISTMAS

I

THERE was once a story-book girl named Betty Leicester, who lived in a small square book bound in scarlet and white. I, who know her better than any one else does, and who know my way about Tideshead, the story-book town, as well as she did, and who have not only made many a visit to her Aunt Barbara and Aunt Mary in their charming old country-house, but have even seen the house in London where she spent the winter: I, who confess to loving Betty a good deal, wish to write a little more about her in this Christmas story. The truth is, that ever since I wrote the first story I have been seeing girls who reminded me of Betty Leicester of Tideshead.

Either they were about the same age or the
same height, or they skipped gayly by me in
a little gown like hers, or I saw a pleased
look or a puzzled look in their eyes which
seemed to bring Betty, my own story-book
girl, right before me.

Now, if anybody has read the book, this
preface will be much more interesting than if
anybody has not. Yet, if I say to all new
acquaintances that Betty was just in the middle of her sixteenth year, and quite in the
middle of girlhood ; that she hated some things
as much as she could, and liked other things
with all her heart, and did not feel pleased
when older people kept saying *don't!* perhaps
these new acquaintances will take the risk of
being friends. Certain things had become
easy just as Betty was leaving Tideshead in
New England, where she had been spending
the summer with her old aunts, so that, having
got used to all the Tideshead liberties and
restrictions, she thought she was leaving the
easiest place in the world ; but when she got

back to London with her father, somehow or other life was very difficult indeed.

She used to wish for London and for her cronies, the Duncans, when she was first in Tideshead; but when she was in England again she found that, being a little nearer to the awful responsibilities of a grown person, she was not only a new Betty, but London — great, busy, roaring, delightful London — was a new London altogether. To say that she felt lonely, and cried one night because she wished to go back to Tideshead and be a village person again, and was homesick for her four-posted bed with the mandarins parading on the curtains, is only to tell the honest truth.

In Tideshead that summer Betty Leicester learned two things which she could not understand quite well enough to believe at first, but which always seem more and more sensible to one as time goes on. The first is that you must be careful what you wish for, because if you wish hard enough you are pretty sure to get it; and the second is, that no two persons can be placed anywhere where one will not be host and the other guest. One will be in a position to give and to help and to show; the other must be the one who depends and receives.

Now, this subject may not seem any clearer to you at first than it did to Betty; but life suddenly became a great deal more interesting, and she felt herself a great deal more important to the rest of the world when she got a little light from these rules. For everybody knows that two of the hardest things in the world are to know what to do and how to behave; to know what one's own duty is in the world and how to get on with other people. What to be and how to behave — these are the questions that every girl has to face; and if somebody answers, "Be good and be polite," it is such a general kind of answer that one throws it away and feels uncomfortable.

I do not remember that I happened to say anywhere in the story that there was a pretty fashion in Tideshead, as summer went on, of calling our friend "Sister Betty." Whether it came from her lamenting that she had no sister, and being kindly adopted by certain friends, or whether there was something in her friendly, affectionate way of treating people, one cannot tell.

II

BETTY LEICESTER, in a new winter gown
which had just been sent home from Liberty's,
with all desirable qualities of color, and a fine
expanse of smocking at the yoke, and some
sprigs of embroidery for ornament in proper
places, was yet an unhappy Betty. In spite
of being not only fine, but snug and warm as
one always feels when cold weather first comes
and one gets into a winter dress, everything
seemed disappointing. The weather was shiv-
ery and dark, the street into which she was
looking was narrow and gloomy, and there
was a moment when Betty thought wistfully
of Tideshead as if there were no December
there, and only the high, clear September sky
that she had left. Somehow, all out-of-door
life appeared to have come to an end, and she
felt as if she were shut into a dark and wintry
prison. Not long before this she had come

from Whitby, the charming red-roofed York-
shire fishing-town that forever climbs the hill
to its gray abbey.   There were flocks of young
people at Whitby that autumn, and Betty had
lived out of doors in pleasant company to her
heart's content, and tramped about the moors
and along the cliffs with gay parties, and
played golf and cricket, and helped to plan
some great excitement or lively excursion for
almost every day.   There is a funny, dancing-
step sort of walk, set to the tune of "Humpty-
Dumpty," which seems to belong with the
Whitby walking-sticks which everybody car-
ries; you lock arms in lines across the road,
and keep step to the gay chant of the dismal
nursery lines, and the faster you go, especially
when you are tired, the more it seems to rest
you (or that's what some people think) in
the long walks home.   Whitby was almost as
good as Tideshead, to which lovely town Betty
now compared every other, even London
itself.

Betty and her father had not yet gone to
housekeeping by themselves (which made them

very happy later on), but they were living in some familiar old Clarges Street lodgings convenient to the Green Park, where Betty could go for a consoling scamper with a new dog called "Toby" because he looked so exactly like the beloved Toby on the cover of "Punch." Betty had spent a whole morning's work upon a proper belled ruff for Toby, who gravely sat up and wore it as if he were conscious of literary responsibilities.

Papa had gone to the British Museum that rainy morning, and was not likely to reappear before the close of day. For a wonder, he was going to dine at home that night. Something very interesting to the scientific world had happened to him during his summer visit to Alaska, and it seemed as if every one of his scientific friends had also made some discovery, or something had happened to each one, which made many talks and dinners and club meetings delightfully important. But most of the London people were in the country; for in England they stay in the hot town until July or August, while all Americans

scatter among green fields or seashore places;
and then spend the gloomy months of the
year in their country houses, when we fly back
to the shelter and music and pictures and
companionship of town life. This all depends
upon the meeting of parliament and other
great reasons; but even Betty Leicester felt
quite left out and lonely in town that dark
day. Her best friends, the Duncans, were at
their great house in Warwickshire. She was
going to stay with them for a month, but not
just yet; while her father was soon going to
pay a short visit to a very great lady indeed
at Danesly Castle, just this side the Border.

This " very great lady indeed" was perfectly
charming to our friend; a smile or a bow
from her was just then more than anything
else to Betty. We all know how perfectly
delightful it is to love some one so much that
we keep dreaming of her a little all the time,
and what happiness it gives when the least
thing one has to do with her is a perfectly
golden joy. Betty loved Mrs. Duncan fondly
and constantly, and she loved Aunt Barbara

with a spark of true enchantment and eager
desire to please ; but for this new friend, for
Lady Mary Danesly (who was Mrs. Duncan's
cousin), there was something quite different
in her heart. As she stood by the window
in Clarges Street she was thinking of this
lovely friend, and wishing for once that she
herself was older, so that perhaps she might
have been asked to come with papa for a
week's visit at Christmas. But Lady Mary
would be busy enough with her great house-
party of distinguished people. Once she had
been so delightful as to say that Betty must
some day come to Danesly with her father,
but of course this could not be the time. Miss
Day, Betty's old governess, who now lived
with her mother in one of the suburbs of
London, was always ready to come to spend a
week or two if Betty were to be left alone,
and it was pleasanter every year to try to
make Miss Day have a good time as well as
to have one one's self; but, somehow, a feeling of having outgrown Miss Day was hard
to bear. They had not much to talk about

except the past, and what they used to do;
and when friendship comes to this alone, it
may be dear, but is never the best sort.

The fog was blowing out of the street, and
the window against which Betty leaned was
suddenly flecked with raindrops. A telegraph
boy came round the corner as if the gust of
wind had brought him, and ran toward the
steps; presently the maid brought in a telegram to Betty, who hastened to open it, as she
was always commissioned to do in her father's
absence. To her surprise it was meant for
herself. She looked at the envelope to make
sure. It was from Lady Mary.

*Can you come to me with your father
next week, dear? I wish for you very much.*

"There's no answer — at least there's no
answer now," said Betty, quite trembling with
excitement and pleasure; "I must see papa
first, but I can't think that he will say no.
He meant to come home for Christmas day
with me, and now we can both stay on."

She hopped about, dancing and skipping, after the door was shut. What a thing it is to have one's wishes come true before one's eyes! And then she asked to have a hansom cab called and for the company of Pagot, who was her maid now; a very nice woman whom Mrs. Duncan had recommended, inasmuch as Betty was older and had thoughts of going to housekeeping. Pagot's sister also was engaged as housemaid, and, strange as it may appear, our Tideshead Betty was to become the mistress of a cook and butler. Pagot herself looked sedate and responsible, but she dearly liked a little change and was finding the day dull. So they started off together toward the British Museum in all the rain, with the shutter of the cab put down and the horse trotting along the shining streets as if he liked it.

III

Mr. Leicester was in the Department of North American Prehistoric Remains, and had a jar of earth before him which he was examining with closest interest. " Here 's a bit of charred bone," he was saying eagerly to a wise-looking old gentleman, " and here 's a funeral bead — just as I expected. This proves my theory of the sacrificial — Why, Betty, what 's the matter? " and he looked startled for a moment. "A telegram? "

" It was so very important, you see, papa," said Betty.

" I thought it was bad news from Tideshead," said Mr. Leicester, looking up at her with a smile after he had read it. " Well, my dear, that 's very nice, and very important too," he added, with a fine twinkle in his eyes. " I shall be going out for a bit of luncheon presently, and I 'll send the answer with great pleasure."

Betty's cheeks were brighter than ever, as if a rosy cloud of joy were shining through. "Now that I'm here, I'll look at the arrowheads; may n't I, papa?" she asked, with great self-possession. "I should like to see if I can find one like mine — I mean my best white one that I found on the river-bank last summer."

Papa nodded, and turned to his jar again. "You may let Pagot go home at one o'clock," he said, "and come back to find me here, and we'll go and have luncheon together. I was thinking of coming home early to get you. We've a house to look at, and it's dull weather for what I wish to do here at the museum. Clear sunshine is the only possible light for this sort of work," he added, turning to the old gentleman, who nodded; and Betty nodded sagely, and skipped away with Pagot, to search among the arrowheads.

She found many white quartz arrowpoints and spearheads like her own treasure. Pagot thought them very dull, and was made rather uncomfortable by the Indian medicine-masks and war-bonnets and evil-looking war-clubs, and openly called it a waste of time for any one to have taken trouble to get all that heathen rubbish together. Such savages and their horrid ways were best forgotten by decent folks, if Pagot might be so bold as to say so. But presently it was luncheon time; and the good soul cheerfully departed, while Betty joined her father, and waited for him as still as a mouse for half an hour, while he and the scientific old gentleman reluctantly said their last words and separated. She had listened to a good deal of their talk about altar fires, and the ceremonies that could be certainly traced in a handful of earth from the site of a temple in the mounds of a buried city; but all her thoughts were of Lady Mary and the pleasures of the next week. She looked again at the telegram, which was much nicer than most telegrams. It was so nice of Lady Mary to have said *dear* in it—just as if she were talking; people did not often say *dear* in a message. "Perhaps some of her guests can't come; but then, everybody likes

to be asked to Danesly," Betty thought.
" And I wonder if I shall dine at table with
the guests; I never have. At any rate, I shall
see Lady Mary often and be with papa. It is
perfectly lovely! I can give her the Indian
basket I brought her, now, before the sweet
grass is all dry."

It was a great delight to be asked to the
holiday party; many a grown person would
be thankful to take Betty's place. For was
not Lady Mary a very great lady indeed, and
one of the most charming women in England? — a famous hostess and assembler of
really delightful people?

"I am going to Danesly on the seventeenth,"
said Betty to herself, with satisfaction.

IV

BETTY and her father had taken a long journey from London. They had been nearly all day in the train, after a breakfast by candle-light; and it was quite dark, except for the light of the full moon in a misty sky, as they drove up the long avenue at Danesly. Pagot was in great spirits; she was to go everywhere with Betty now, being used to the care of young ladies, and more being expected of this young lady than in the past. Pagot had been at Danesly before with the Duncans, and had many friends in the household.

Mr. Leicester was walking across the fields by a path he well knew from the little station, with a friend and fellow guest whom they had met at Durham. This path was much shorter than the road, so that papa was sure of reaching the house first; but Betty felt a little lonely, being tired, and shy of meeting a great

bright houseful of people quite by herself, in
case papa should loiter. But suddenly the
carriage stopped, and the footman jumped
down and opened the door. "My lady is
walking down to meet you, miss," he said;
"she's just ahead of us, coming down the
avenue." And Betty flew like a pigeon to
meet her dear friend. The carriage drove
on and left them together under the great
trees, walking along together over the beautiful tracery of shadows. Suddenly Lady Mary
felt the warmth of Betty's love for her and
her speechless happiness as she had not felt
it before, and she stopped, looking so tall and
charming, and put her two arms round Betty,
and hugged her to her heart.

"My dear little girl!" she said for the
second time; and then they walked on, and
still Betty could not say anything for sheer
joy. "Now I'm going to tell you something
quite in confidence," said the hostess of the
great house, which showed its dim towers and
scattered lights beyond the leafless trees. "I
had been wishing to have you come to me,

but I should not have thought this the best time for a visit; later on, when the days will be longer, I shall be able to have much more time to myself. But an American friend of mine, Mr. Banfield, who is a friend of your papa's, I believe, wrote to ask if he might bring his young daughter, whom he had taken from school in New York for a holiday. It seemed a difficult problem for the first moment," and Lady Mary gave a funny little laugh. " I did not know quite what to do with her just now, as I should with a grown person. And then I remembered that I might ask you to help me, Betty dear. You know that the Duncans always go for a Christmas visit to their grandmother in Devon."

" I was so glad to come," said Betty warmly ; " it was nicer than anything else."

"I am a little afraid of young American girls, you understand," said Lady Mary gayly ; and then, taking a solemn tone : " Yes, you need n't laugh, Miss Betty ! But you know all about what they like, don't you? and so I am sure we can make a bit of pleasure

together, and we'll be fellow hostesses, won't
we? We must find some time every day for
a little talking over of things quite by ourselves. I've put you next your father's
rooms, and to-morrow Miss Banfield will be
near by, and you're to dine in my little morning-room to-night. I'm so glad good old
Pagot is with you; she knows the house perfectly well. I hope you will soon feel at
home. Why, this is almost like having a girl
of my very own," said Lady Mary wistfully,
as they began to go up the great steps and
into the hall, where the butler and other
splendid personages of the household stood
waiting. Lady Mary was a tall, slender figure
in black, with a beautiful head; and she carried herself with great spirit and grace. She
had wrapped some black lace about her head
and shoulders, and held it gathered with one
hand at her throat.

"I must fly to the drawing-room now, and
then go to dress for dinner; so good-night,
darling," said this dear lady, whom Betty had
always longed to be nearer to and to know

"I WAS SO GLAD TO COME"

better. " To-morrow you must tell me all about your summer in New England," she said, looking over her shoulder as she went one way and Betty another, with Pagot and a footman who carried the small luggage from the carriage. How good and kind she had been to come to meet a young stranger who might feel lonely, and as if there were no place for her in the great strange house in the first minute of her arrival. And Betty Leicester quite longed to see Miss Banfield and to help her to a thousand pleasures at once for Lady Mary's sake.

V

SOMEBODY has said that there are only a very few kinds of people in the world, but that they are put into all sorts of places and conditions. The minute Betty Leicester looked at Edith Banfield next day she saw that she was a little like Mary Beck, her own friend and Tideshead neighbor. The first thought was one of pleasure, and the second was a fear that the new "Becky" would not have a good time at Danesly. It was the morning after Betty's own arrival. That first evening she had her dinner alone, and afterward was reading and resting after her journey in Lady Mary's own little sitting-room, which was next her own room. When Pagot came up from her own hasty supper and "crack" with her friends to look after Betty, and to unpack, she had great tales to tell of the large and noble company assembled at Danesly House.

"They 're dining in the great banquet hall itself," she said with pride. "Lady Mary looks a queen at the head of the table, with the French prince beside her and the great Earl of Seacliff at the other side," said Pagot proudly. "I took a look from the old musicians' gallery, miss, as I came along, and it was a fine sight, indeed. Lady Mary's own maid, as I have known well these many years, was telling me the names of the strangers." Pagot was very proud of her own knowledge of fine people.

Betty asked if it was far to the gallery; and, finding that it was quite near the part of the house where they were, she went out with Pagot along the corridors with their long rows of doors, and into the musicians' gallery, where they found themselves at a delightful point of view. Danesly Castle had been built at different times; the banquet-hall itself was very old and stately, with a high, carved roof. There were beautiful old hangings and banners where the walls and roof met, and lower down were spread great tapes-

tries. There was a huge fire blazing in the
deep fireplace at the end, and screens before
it; the long table twinkled with candle-light,
and the gay company sat about it. Betty
looked first for papa, and saw him sitting
beside Lady Dimdale, who was a great friend
of his; then she looked for Lady Mary, who
was at the head between the two gentlemen of
whom Pagot had spoken. She was still dressed
in black lace, but with many diamonds sparkling at her throat, and she looked as sweet
and quiet and self-possessed as if there were
no great entertainment at all. The men-ser-
vants in their handsome livery moved quickly
to and fro, as if they were actors in a play.
The people at the table were talking and
laughing, and the whole scene was so pleasant,
so gay and friendly, that Betty wished, for
almost the first time, that she were grown up
and dining late, to hear all the delightful talk.
She and Pagot were like swallows high under
the eaves of the great room. Papa looked
really boyish, so many of the men were older
than he. There were twenty at table; and

Pagot said, as Betty counted them, that many others were expected the next day. You could imagine the great festivals of an older time as you looked down from the gallery. In the gallery itself there were quaint little heavy wooden stools for the musicians: the harpers and fiddlers and pipers who had played for so many generations of gay dancers, for whom the same lights had flickered, and over whose heads the old hangings had waved. You felt as if you were looking down at the past. Betty and Pagot closed the narrow door of the gallery softly behind them, and our friend went back to her own bedroom, where there was a nice fire, and nearly fell asleep before it, while Pagot was getting the last things unpacked and ready for the night.

VI

THE next day at about nine o'clock Lady
Mary came through her morning-room and
tapped at the door. Betty was just ready and
very glad to say good-morning. The sun was
shining, and she had been leaning out upon
the great stone window-sill looking down the
long slopes of the country into the wintry
mists. Lady Mary looked out too, and took
a long breath of the fresh, keen air. "It's a
good day for hunting," she said, "and for
walking. I'm going down to breakfast, because I have planned for an idle day. I
thought we might go down together if you
were ready."

Betty's heart was filled with gratitude ; it
was so very kind of her hostess to remember
that it would be difficult for the only girl in
the house party to come alone to breakfast for
the first time. They went along the corridor

and down the great staircase, past the portraits
and the marble busts and figures on the land-
ings.   There were two or three ladies in the
great hall at the foot, with an air of being
very early, and some gentlemen who were
going fox hunting ; and after Betty had spoken
with Lady Dimdale, whom she knew, they
sauntered into the breakfast-room, where they
found some other people ; and papa and Betty
had a word together and then sat down side
by side to their muffins and their eggs and
toast and marmalade.   It was not a bit like
a Tideshead company breakfast.   Everybody
jumped up if he wished for a plate, or for
more jam, or some cold game, which was on
the sideboard with many other things.   The
company of servants had disappeared, and it
was all as unceremonious as if the breakfasters
were lunching out of doors.   There was not
a long tableful like that of the night before;
many of the guests were taking their tea and
coffee in their own rooms.

By the time breakfast was done, Betty had
begun to forget herself as if she were quite at

home. She stole an affectionate glance now
and then at Lady Mary, and had fine bits of
talk with her father, who had spent a charming evening and now told Betty something
about it, and how glad he was to have her see
their fellow guests. When he went hurrying
away to join the hunt, Betty was sure that she
knew exactly what to do with herself. It
would take her a long time to see the huge
old house and the picture gallery, where there
were some very famous paintings, and the
library, about which papa was always so en-
thusiastic. Lady Mary was to her more interesting than anybody else, and she wished
especially to do something for Lady Mary.
Aunt Barbara had helped her niece very much
one day in Tideshead when she talked about
her own experience in making visits and going
much into company. "The best thing you
can do," she said, "is to do everything you
can to help your hostess. Don't wait to see
what is going to be done for you, but try to
help entertain your fellow guests and to make
the moment pleasant, and you will be sure to

enjoy yourself and to find your hostess wishing you to come again. Always do the things that will help your hostess." Our friend thought of this sage advice now, but it was at a moment when every one else was busy talking, and they were all going on to the great library except two or three late breakfasters who were still at the table. Aunt Barbara had also said that when there was nothing else to do, your plain duty was to entertain yourself; and, having a natural gift for this, Betty wandered off into a corner and found a new " Punch " and some of the American magazines on a little table close by the window-seat. After a while she happened to hear some one ask : " What time is Mr. Banfield coming ? "

" By the eleven o'clock train," said Lady Mary. " I am just watching for the carriage that is to fetch him. Look ; you can see it first between the two oaks there to the left. It is an awkward time to get to a strange house, poor man ; but they were in the South and took a night train that is very slow. Mr.

Banfield's daughter is with him, and my dear friend Betty, who knows what American girls like best, is kindly going to help me entertain her."

" Oh, really ! " said one of the ladies, looking up and smiling as if she had been wondering just what Betty was for, all alone in the grown-up house party. " Really, that 's very nice. But I might have seen that you are Mr. Leicester's daughter. It was very stupid of me, my dear ; you 're quite like him — oh, quite ! "

" I have seen you with the Duncans, have I not ? " asked some one else, with great interest. " Why, fancy ! " said this friendly person, who was named the Honorable Miss Northumberland, a small, eager little lady in spite of her solemn great name, — " fancy ! you must be an American too. I should have thought you quite an English girl."

" Oh, no, indeed," said Betty. " Indeed, I 'm quite American, except for living in England a very great deal." She was ready to go on and say much more, but she had been taught to say as little about herself as she possibly could, since general society cares little for knowledge that is given it too easily, especially about strangers and one's self!

"There's the carriage now," said Lady Mary, as she went away to welcome the guests. "Poor souls! they will like to get to their rooms as soon as possible," she said hospitably; but although the elder ladies did not stir, Betty deeply considered the situation, and then, with a happy impulse, hurried after her hostess. It was a long way about, through two or three rooms and the great hall to the entrance; but Betty overtook Lady Mary just as she reached the great door, going forward in the most hospitable, charming way to meet the new-comers. She did not seem to have seen Betty at all.

The famous lawyer, Mr. Banfield, came quickly up the steps, and after him, more slowly, came his daughter, whom he seemed quite to forget.

A footman was trying to take her wraps and traveling-bag, but she clung fast to them, and looked up apprehensively toward Lady Mary.

Betty was very sympathetic, and was sure that it was a trying moment, and she ran down to meet Miss Banfield, and happened to be so fortunate as to catch her just as she was tripping over her dress upon the high stone step. Mr. Banfield himself was well known in London, and was a great favorite in society ; but at first sight his daughter's self-conscious manners struck one as being less interesting. She was a pretty girl, but she wore a pretentious look, which was further borne out by very noticeable clothes — not at all the right things to travel in at that hour ; but, as has long ago been said, Betty saw at once the likeness to her Tideshead friend and comrade, Mary Beck, and opened her heart to take the stranger in. It was impossible not to be reminded of the day when Mary Beck came to call in Tideshead, with her best hat and bird-of-paradise feather, and they both felt so awkward and miserable.

" Did you have a very tiresome journey ? "

Betty was asking as they reached the top of
the steps at last; but Edith Banfield's reply
was indistinct, and the next moment Lady
Mary turned to greet her young guest cordially. Betty felt that she was a little dis-
mayed, and was all the more eager to have
the young compatriot's way made easy.

"Did you have a tiresome journey?" asked
Lady Mary, in her turn; but the reply was
quite audible now.

"Oh, yes," said Edith. "It was awfully
cold — oh, awfully! — and so smoky and
horrid and dirty! I thought we never should
get here, with changing cars in horrid stations,
and everything," she said, telling all about it.

"Oh, that was too bad," said Betty, rush-
ing to the rescue, while Lady Mary walked
on with Mr. Banfield. Edith Banfield talked
on in an excited, persistent way to Betty,
after having finally yielded up her bag to the
footman, and looking after him somewhat
anxiously. "It's a splendid big house, is n't
it?" she whispered; "but awfully solemn
looking. I suppose there's another part

where they live, is n't there? Have you been
here before? Are you English?"

"I'm Betty Leicester," said Betty, in an
undertone. "No, I have n't been here before;
but I have known Lady Mary for a long time
in London. I'm an American, too."

"You are n't, really!" exclaimed Edith.
"Why, you must have been over here a good
many times, or something" — She cast a
glance at Betty's plain woolen gear, and recog-
nized the general comfortable appearance of
the English schoolgirl. Edith herself was
very fine in silk attire, with much fur trim-
ming and a very expensive hat. "Well, I'm
awfully glad you're here," she said, with a
satisfied sigh; "you know all about it better
than I do, and can tell me what to put on."

"Oh, yes, indeed," said Betty cheerfully;
"and there are lots of nice things to do. We
can see the people, and then there are all the
pictures and the great conservatories, and the
stables and dogs and everything. I've been
waiting to see them with you; and we can
ride every day, if you like; and papa says

it's a perfectly delightful country for walking."

"I hate to walk," said Edith frankly.

"Oh, what a pity," lamented Betty, a good
deal dashed. She was striving against a very
present disappointment, but still the fact could
not be overlooked that Edith Banfield looked
like Mary Beck. Now, Mary also was apt to
distrust all strangers and to take suspicious
views of life, and she had little enthusiasm;
but Betty knew and loved her loyalty and
really good heart. She felt sometimes as
if she tried to walk in tight shoes when
"Becky's" opinions had to be considered;
but Becky's world had grown wider month by
month, and she loved her very much. Edith
Banfield was very pretty; that was a comfort,
and though Betty might never like her as she
did Mary Beck, she meant more than ever to
help her to have a good visit.

Lady Mary appeared again, having given
Mr. Banfield into the young footman's charge.
She looked at Sister Betty for an instant with
an affectionate, amused little smile, and kept

one hand on her shoulder as she talked for a minute pleasantly with the new guest.

A maid appeared to take Edith to her room, and Lady Mary patted Betty's shoulder as they parted. They did not happen to have time for a word together again all day.

By luncheon time the two girls were very good friends, and Betty knew all about the new-comer; and in spite of a succession of minor disappointments, the acquaintance promised to be very pleasant. Poor Edith Banfield, like poor Betty, had no mother, but Edith had spent several years already at a large boarding-school. She was taking this journey by way of vacation, and was going back after the Christmas holidays. She was a New-Yorker, and she hated the country, and loved to stay in foreign hotels. This was the first time she had ever paid a visit in England, except to some American friends who had a villa on the Thames, which Edith had found quite dull. She had not been taught either to admire or to enjoy very much, which seemed to make her schooling count for but

little so far ; but she adored her father and
his brilliant wit in a most lovely way, and
with this affection and pride Betty could
warmly sympathize. Edith longed to please
her father in every possible fashion, and
secretly confessed that she did not always suc-
ceed, in a way that touched Betty's heart. It
was hard to know exactly how to please the
busy man ; he was apt to show only a mild
interest in the new clothes which at present
were her chief joy; perhaps she was always
making the mistake of not so much trying to
please him as to make him pleased with herself, which is quite a different thing.

VII

THERE was an anxious moment on Betty's part when Edith Banfield summoned her to decide upon what dress should be worn for the evening. Pagot, whom Betty had asked to go and help her new friend, was wearing a disapproving look, and two or three fine French dresses were spread out for inspection.

" Why, are n't you going to dress? " asked Edith. " I was afraid you were all ready to go down, but I could n't think what to put on."

" I 'm all dressed," said Betty, with surprise. " Oh, what lovely gowns! But we " — she suddenly foresaw a great disappointment — " we need n't go down yet, you know, Edith; we are not out, and dinner is n't like luncheon here in England. We can go down afterward, if we like, and hear the songs, but we girls never go to dinner when it 's a great dinner

like this. I think it is much better fun to
stay away ; at least, I always have thought so
until last night, and then it did really look
very pleasant," she frankly added. " Why,
I 'm not sixteen, and you 're only a little past,
you know." But there lay a grown-up young
lady's evening gowns as if to confute all
Betty's arguments.

" How awfully stupid ! " said Edith, with
great scorn. "Nursery tea for anybody like
us ! " and she turned to look at Betty's dress,
which was charming enough in its way, and
made in very pretty girlish fashion. " I should
think they 'd make you wear a white pina-
fore," said Edith ungraciously; but Betty,
who had been getting a little angry, thought
this so funny that she laughed and felt much
better.

" I wear muslins for very best," she said
serenely. " Why, of course we 'll go down
after dinner and stay a while before we say
good-night; they 'll be out before half-past
nine, — I mean the ladies, — and we 'll be
there in the drawing-room. Oh, is n't that

blue gown a beauty! I wish I had put on my best muslin, Pagot."

"You look very suitable, Miss Betty," said Pagot stiffly. Pagot was very old-fashioned, and Edith made a funny little face at Betty behind her back.

The two girls had a delightful dinner together in the morning-room next Betty's own, and Edith's good humor was quite restored. She had had a good day, on the whole, and the picture galleries and conservatories had not failed to please by their splendors and delights. After they had finished their dessert, Betty, as a great surprise, offered the hospitalities of the musicians' gallery, and they sped along the corridors and up the stairs in great spirits, Betty leading the way. "Now, don't upset the little benches," she whispered, as she opened the narrow door out of the dark passage, and presently their two heads were over the edge of the gallery. They leaned boldly out, for nobody would think of looking up.

The great hall was even gayer and brighter

than it had looked the night before. The
lights and colors shone, there were new people
at table, and much talk was going on. The
butler and his men were more military than
ever; it was altogether a famous, much-dia-
monded dinner company, and Lady Mary
looked quite magnificent at the head.

"It looks pretty," whispered Edith; "but
how dull it sounds! I don't believe that they
are having a bit of a good time. At home,
you know, there's such a noise at a party.
What a splendid big room!"

"People never talk loud when they get
together in England," said Betty. "They
never make that awful chatter that we do at
home. Just four or five people who come to
tea in Tideshead can make one another's ears
ache. I couldn't get used to it last summer;
Aunt Barbara was almost the only tea-party
person in Tideshead who didn't get scream-
ing."

"Oh, I do think it's splendid!" said Edith
wistfully. "I wish we were down there. I
wish there was a little gallery lower down.

There's Lord Dunwater, who sat next me at luncheon. Who's that next your father?"

There was a little noise behind the eager girls, and they turned quickly. A tall boy had joined them, who seemed much disturbed at finding any one in the gallery, which seldom had a visitor. Edith stood up, and seemed an alarmingly tall and elegant young lady in the dim light. Betty, who was as tall, was nothing like so imposing to behold at that moment; but the new-comer turned to make his escape.

"Don't go away," Betty begged, seeing his alarm, and wondering who he could be. "There's plenty of room to look. Don't go." And thereupon the stranger came forward.

He was a handsome fellow, dressed in Eton clothes. He was much confused, and said nothing; and, after a look at the company below, during which the situation became more embarrassing to all three, he turned to go away.

"Are you staying in the house, too?"

A TALL BOY HAD JOINED THEM

asked Betty timidly; it was so very awkward.

"I just came," said the boy, who now appeared to be a very nice fellow indeed. They
had left the musicians' gallery,—nobody knew
why,—and now stood outside in the corridor.

"I just came," he repeated. "I walked
over from the station across the fields. I 'm
Lady Mary's nephew, you know. She 's not
expecting me. I had my supper in the housekeeper's room. I was going on a week's
tramp in France with my old tutor, just to
get rid of Christmas parties and things; but
he strained a knee at football, and we had to
give it up, and so I came here for the holidays.
There was nothing else to do," he explained
ruefully. "What a lot of people my aunt's
got this year!"

"It 's very nice," said Betty cordially.

"It 's beastly slow, *I* think," said the boy.
"I like it much better when my aunt and I
have the place to ourselves. Oh, no; that 's
not what I mean!" he said, blushing crimson
as both the girls laughed. "Only we have

jolly good times by ourselves, you know; no
end of walks and rides; and we fish if the
water's right.   You ought to see my aunt
cast a fly."

"She's perfectly lovely, is n't she?" said
Betty, in a tone which made them firm
friends at once.   "We're going down to
the drawing-room soon; would n't you like
to come?"

"Yes," said the boy slowly.   "It 'll be
fun to surprise her.   And I saw Lady Dimdale
at dinner.   I like Lady Dimdale awfully."

"So does papa," said Betty; "oh, so very
much! — next to Lady Mary and Mrs. Duncan."

"You 're Betty Leicester, are n't you?
Oh, I know you now," said the boy, turning
toward her with real friendliness.   "I danced
with you at the Duncans', at a party, just
before I first went to Eton, — oh, ever so
long ago! — you won't remember it; and I 've
seen you once besides, at their place in Warwickshire, you know.   I 'm Warford, you
know."

"Why, of course," said Betty, with great pleasure. "It puzzled me; I could n't think at first, but you 've quite grown up since then. How we used to dance when we were little things! Do you like it now?"

"No, I hate it," said Warford coldly, and they all three laughed. Edith was walking alongside, feeling much left out of the conversation, though Warford had been stealing glances at her.

"Oh, I am so sorry — I did n't think," Betty exclaimed in her politest manner. "Miss Banfield, this is Lord Warford. I did n't mean to be rude, but you were a great surprise, were n't you?" and they all laughed again, as young people will. Just then they reached the door of Lady Mary's morning-room; the girls' dessert was still on the table, and, being properly invited, Warford began to eat the rest of the fruit. "One never gets quite enough grapes," said Warford, who was evidently suffering the constant hunger of a rapidly growing person.

Edith Banfield certainly looked very pretty,

both her companions thought so; but they
felt much more at home with each other. It
seemed as if she were a great deal older than
they, in her fine evening gown. Warford
was very admiring and very polite, but Betty
and he were already plunged into the deep
intimacy of true fellowship. Edith got im-
patient before they were ready to go down-
stairs, but at last they all started down the
great staircase, and had just settled themselves in the drawing-room when the ladies
began to come in.

"Why, Warford, my dear!" said Lady
Mary, with great delight, as he met her and
kissed her twice, as if they were quite by
themselves; then he turned and spoke to
Lady Dimdale, who was just behind, still
keeping Lady Mary's left hand in his own.
Warford looked taller and more manly than
ever in the bright light, and he was recog-
nized warmly by nearly all the ladies, being
not only a fine fellow, but the heir of Danesly
and great possessions besides, so that he stood
for much that was interesting, even if he had

not been interesting himself. Betty and Edith looked on with pleasure, and presently Lady Mary came toward them.

" I am so glad that you came down," she said; "and how nice of you to bring Warford! He usually objects so much that I believe you have found some new way to make it easy. I suppose it is dull when he is by himself. Mr. Frame is here, and has promised to sing by and by. He and Lady Dimdale have practiced some duets — their voices are charming together. I hope that you will not go up until afterward, no matter how late."

Betty, who had been sitting when Lady Mary came toward her, had risen at once to meet her, without thinking about it; but Edith Banfield still sat in her low chair, feeling stiff and uncomfortable, while Lady Mary did not find it easy to talk down at her or to think of anything to say. All at once it came to Edith's mind to follow Betty's example, and they all three stood together talking cheerfully until Lady Mary had to go to her other guests.

"Is n't she lovely!" said Edith, with all the ardor that Betty could wish. "I don't feel a bit afraid of her, as I thought I should."

"She takes such dear trouble," said Betty, warmly. "She never forgets anybody. Some grown persons behave as if you ought to be ashamed of not being older, and as if you were going to bore them if they did n't look out." At this moment Warford came back most loyally from the other side of the room, and presently some gentlemen made their appearance, and the delightful singing began. Betty, who loved music, sat and listened like a quiet young robin in her red dress, and her father, who looked at her happy, dreaming face, was sure that there never had been a dearer girl in the world. Lady Mary looked at her too, and was really full of wonder, because in some way Betty had managed with simple friendliness to make her shy nephew quite forget himself, and to give some feeling of belongingness to Edith Banfield, who would have felt astray by herself in a strange English house.

VIII

THE days flew by until Christmas, and the weather kept clear and bright, without a bit of rain or gloom, which was quite delightful and wonderful in that northern country. The older guests hunted or drove or went walking. There were excursions of every sort for those who liked them, and sometimes the young people joined in what was going on, and sometimes Betty and Edith and Warford made fine plans of their own. It proved that Edith had spent much time with the family of her uncle, who was an army officer; and at the Western army posts she had learned to ride with her cousins, who were excellent riders and insisted upon her joining them. So Edith could share many pleasures of this sort at Danesly, and she was so pretty and gay that people liked her a good deal; and presently some of the house party had gone,

and some new guests came, and the two girls
and Warford were unexpected helpers in their
entertainment. Sometimes they dined down-
stairs now, when no one was asked from outside; and every day it seemed pleasanter and
more homelike to stay at Danesly. There
were one or two other great houses in the
neighborhood where there were also house
parties in the gay holiday season, and so
Betty and Edith saw a great deal of the
world in one way and another; and Lady
Mary remembered that girls were sometimes
lonely, as they grew up, and was very good
to them, teaching them, in quiet ways, many
a thing belonging to manners and getting on
with other people, that they would be glad to
know all their life long.

"Don't talk about yourself," she said once,
"and you won't half so often think of yourself, and then you are sure to be happy."
And again: "My old friend, Mrs. Procter,
used to say, ' *Never explain, my dear. People don't care a bit.*' "

Warford was more at home in the hunting

BETTY, EDITH AND WARFORD

field than in the house ; but the young people
saw much of each other. He took a great
deal of trouble, considering his usual fashion,
to be nice to the two girls ; and so one day,
when Betty went to find him, he looked up
eagerly to see what she wanted. ·Warford
was busy in the gun room, with the parts of
a gun which he had taken to pieces. There
was nobody else there at that moment, and
the winter sun was shining in along the
floor.

" Warford," Betty began, with an air of
great confidence, " what can we do for a bit
of fun at Christmas ? "

Warford looked up at her over his shoulder,
a little bewildered. He was just this side
of sixteen, like Betty herself ; sometimes he
seemed manly, and sometimes very boyish, as
happened that day. " I 'm in for anything
you like," he said, after a moment's reflec-
tion. " What 's on ? "

" If we give up dining with the rest, I can
think of a great plan," said Betty, shining
with enthusiasm. " There 's the old gallery,

you know. Could n't we have some music there, as they used in old times?"

"My aunt would like it awfully," exclaimed Warford, letting his gunstock drop with a thump. "I 'd rather do anything than sit all through the dinner. Somebody 'd be sure to make a row about me, and I should feel like getting into a burrow. I 'll play the fiddle: what did you mean? — singing, or what? If we had it Christmas Eve, we might have the Christmas waits, you know."

"*Fancy!*" said Betty, in true English fashion; and then they both laughed.

"The waits are pretty silly," said Warford. "They were better than usual last year, though. Mr. Macalister, the schoolmaster, is a good musician, and he trained them well. He plays the flute and the cornet. Why not see what we can do ourselves first, and perhaps let them sing last? They 'd be disappointed not to come at midnight under the windows, you know," said Warford considerately. "We 'll go down and ask the schoolmaster after hours, and we 'll think what we

can do ourselves. One of the grooms has a
lovely tenor voice. I heard him singing 'The
Bonny Ivy Tree' like a flute only yesterday,
so he must know more of those other old
things that Aunt Mary likes."

"We need n't have much music," said
Betty. "The people at dinner will not listen
long, — they'll want to talk. But if we sing
a Christmas song all together, and have the
flute and fiddle, you know, Warford, it would
be very pretty — like an old-fashioned choir,
such as there used to be in Tideshead. We'll
sing things that everybody knows, because
everybody likes old songs best. I wish Mary
Beck was here; but Edith sings — she told
me so; and don't you know how we sang
some nice things together, the other day upon
the moor, when we were coming home from
the hermit's-cell ruins?"

Warford nodded, and picked up his gunstock.

"I'm your man," he said soberly. "Let's
dress up whoever sings, with wigs and ruffles
and things. And then there are queer trum-

pets and viols in that collection of musical instruments in the music-room. Some of us can make believe play them."

" A procession! a procession!" exclaimed Betty. " What do you say to a company with masks to come right into the great hall, and walk round the table three times, singing and playing? Lady Dimdale knows everything about music; I mean to ask her. I'll go and find her now."

"I'll come, too," said Warford, with delightful sympathy. " I saw her a while ago writing in the little book-room off the library."

IX

IT was Christmas at last; and all the three young people had been missing since before luncheon in a most mysterious manner. But Betty Leicester, who came in late and flushed, managed to sit next her father; and he saw at once, being well acquainted with Betty, that some great affair was going on. She was much excited, and her eyes were very bright, and there was such a great secret that Mr. Leicester could do no less than ask to be let in, and be gayly refused and hushed, lest somebody else should know there was a secret, too. Warford, who appeared a little later, looked preternaturally solemn, and Edith alone behaved as if nothing were going to happen. She was as grown-up as possible, and chattered away about the delights of New York with an old London barrister who was Lady Mary's uncle, and Warford's guardian, and chief adviser to the great Danesly estates. Edith was so pretty and talked so brightly that the old gentleman looked as amused and happy as possible.

"He may be thinking that she's coming down to dinner, but he'll look for her in vain," said Betty, who grew gayer herself.

"Not coming to dinner?" asked papa, with surprise; at which Betty gave him so stern a glance that he was more careful to avoid even the appearance of secrets from that time on; and they talked together softly about dear old Tideshead, and Aunt Barbara, and all the household, and wondered if the great Christmas box from London had arrived safely and gone up the river by the packet, just as Betty herself had done six or seven months before. It made her a little home-sick, even there in the breakfast-room at Danesly, — even with papa at her side, and Lady Mary smiling back if she looked up, — to think of the dear old house, and of Serena and Letty, and how they would all be think-ing of her at Christmas time.

The great hall was gay with holly and Christmas greens. It was snowing outside for the first time that year, and the huge fireplace was full of logs blazing and snapping in a splendidly cheerful way. Dinner was to be earlier than usual. A great festivity was going on in the servants' hall; and when Warford went out with Lady Mary to cut the great Christmas cake and have his health drunk, Betty and Edith went too; and everybody stood up and cheered, and cried, " Merry Christmas ! Merry Christmas ! and God bless you ! " in the most hearty fashion. It seemed as if all the holly in the Danesly woods had been brought in — as if Christmas had never been so warm and friendly and generous in a great house before. Christmas eve had begun, and cast its lovely charm and enchantment over everybody's heart. Old dislikes were forgotten between the guests; at Christmas time it is easy to say kind words that are hard to say all the rest of the year; at Christmas time one loves his neighbor and thinks better of him; Christmas love and good-will come and fill the heart whether one beckons them or no. Betty had spent some lonely Christmases in her short life, as all the rest of us have done; and perhaps for this reason the keeping of the great day at Danesly in such happy company, in such splendor and warm-heartedness of the old English fashion, seemed a kind of royal Christmas to her young heart. Everybody was so kind and charming.

Lady Dimdale, who had entered with great enthusiasm into the Christmas plans, caught her after luncheon and kissed her, and held her hand like an elder sister as they walked away. It would have been very hard to keep things from Lady Mary herself; but that dear lady had many ways to turn her eyes and her thoughts, and so many secret plots of her own to keep in hand at this season, that she did not suspect what was going on in a distant room of the old south wing (where Warford still preserved some of his boyish collections of birds' eggs and other plunder), of which he kept the only key. There was

a steep staircase that led down to a door in
the courtyard; and by this Mr. Macalister,
the schoolmaster, had come and gone, and the
young groom of the tenor voice, and five or
six others, men and girls, who could either
sing or play. It was the opposite side of
the house from Lady Mary's own rooms, and
nobody else would think anything strange of
such comings and goings. Pagot and some
friendly maids helped with the costumes.
They had practiced their songs twice in the
schoolmaster's own house at nightfall, down
at the edge of the village by the church; and
so everything was ready, with the help of
Lady Dimdale and of Mrs. Drum, the housekeeper, who would always do everything that
Warford asked her, and be heartily pleased
besides.

So Lady Mary did not know what was
meant until after her Christmas guests were
seated, and the old vicar had said grace, and
all the great candelabra were lit, high on the
walls between the banners and flags, and
among the staghorns and armor lower down,

and there were lights even in the old musicians' gallery, which she could see as she sat with her back to the painted leather screen that hid the fireplace.   Suddenly there was a sound of violins and a bass-viol and a flute from the gallery, and a sound of voices singing — the fresh young voices of Warford and Betty and Edith and their helpers, who sang a beautiful old Christmas song, so unexpected, so lovely, that the butler stopped halfway from the sideboard with the wine, and the footmen stood listening where they were, with whatever they had in hand.   The guests at dinner looked up in surprise, and Lady Dimdale nodded across at Mr. Leicester because they both knew it was Betty's plan coming true in this delightful way.   And fresh as the voices were, the look of the singers was even better, for you could see from below that all the musicians were in quaint costume.   The old schoolmaster stood in the middle as leader, with a splendid powdered wig and gold-laced coat, and all the rest wore coats and gowns of velvet and brocade from the old house's store of treasures. They made a charming picture against the wall with its dark tapestry, and Lady Dimdale felt proud of her own part in the work.

There was a cry of delight from below as the first song ended. Betty in the far corner of the gallery could see Lady Mary looking up so pleased and happy and holding her dear white hands high as she applauded with the rest. Nobody knew better than Lady Mary that dinners are sometimes dull, and that even a Christmas dinner is none the worse for a little brightening. So Betty had helped her in great as well as in little things, and she blessed the child from her heart. Then the dinner went on, and so did the music ; it was a pretty programme, and before anybody had dreamed of being tired of it the sound ceased and the gallery was empty.

After a while, when dessert was soon coming in, and the Christmas pudding with its flaming fire might be expected at any moment, there was a pause and a longer delay than usual in the serving. People were talking busily about the long table, and hardly noticed this until with loud knocking and sound of music, old Bond, the butler, made his appearance, with an assistant on either hand, bearing the plum pudding aloft in solemn majesty, the flames rising merrily from the huge platter. Behind him came a splendid retinue of the musicians, singing and playing; every one carried some picturesque horn or trumpet or stringed instrument from Lady Mary's collection, and those who sang also made believe to play in the interludes. Behind these were all the men in livery, two and two; and so they went round and round the table until at last Warford slipped into his seat, and the pudding was put before him with great state, while the procession waited. The tall shy boy forgot himself and his shyness, and was full of the gayety of his pleasure. The costumes were all somewhat fine for Christmas choristers, and the young heir wore a magnificent combination of garments that had belonged to noble peers his

ancestors, and was pretty nearly too splendid
to be well seen without smoked glass. For
the first time in his life he felt a brave happiness in belonging to Danesly, and in the
thought that Danesly would really belong to
him ; he looked down the long room at Lady
Mary, and loved her as he never had before,
and understood things all in a flash, and made
a vow to be a good fellow and to stand by
her so that she should never, never feel alone
or overburdened again.

Betty and Edith and the good schoolmaster (who was splendid in his white wig,
and a great addition to the already brilliant
company) took their own places, which were
quickly made, and dessert went on ; the rest
of the musicians had been summoned away
by Mrs. Drum, the housekeeper, — all these
things having been planned beforehand. And
then it was soon time for the ladies to go to
the drawing-room, and Betty, feeling a little
tired and out of breath with so much excitement, slipped away by herself and to her
own thoughts ; of Lady Mary, who would be

busy with her guests, but still more of papa, who must be waited for until he came to join the ladies, when she could have a talk with him before they said good-night. It was perfectly delightful that everything had gone off so well. Lady Dimdale had known just what to do about everything, and Edith, who had grown nicer every day, had sung as well as Mary Beck (she had Becky's voice as well as her look, and had told Betty it was the best time she ever had in her life); and Warford had been so nice and had looked so handsome, and Lady Mary was so pleased because he was not shy and had not tried to hide or be grumpy, as he usually did. Betty liked Warford better than any boy she had ever seen, except Harry Foster in Tideshead. They would be sure to like each other, and perhaps they might meet some day. Harry's life of care and difficulty made him seem older than Warford, upon whom everybody had always showered all the good things he could be persuaded to take.

X

BETTY was all by herself, walking up and down in the long picture gallery. There were lights here and there in the huge, shadowy room, but the snow had ceased falling out of doors, and the moon was out and shone brightly in at the big windows with their leaded panes. She felt very happy. It was so pleasant to see how everybody cared about papa, and thought him so delightful. She had never seen him in his place with such a company of people, or known so many of his friends together before. It was so good of Lady Mary to have let her come with papa. They would have so many things to talk over together when they got back to town.

The old pictures on the wall were watching Miss Betty Leicester of Tideshead as she walked past them through the squares of moonlight, and into the dim candle-light and out to the moonlight again. It was cooler in the gallery than in the great hall, but not too cold, and it was quiet and still. She was dressed in an ancient pink brocade, with fine old lace, that had come out of a camphor-wood chest in one of the storerooms, and she still held a little old-fashioned lute carefully under her arm. Suddenly one of the doors opened, and Lady Mary came in and crossed the moonlight square toward her.

" So here you are, darling," she said. " I missed you, and every one is wondering where you are. I asked Lady Dimdale, and she remembered that she saw you come this way."

Lady Mary was holding Betty, lace and lute and all, in her arms, and then she kissed her in a way that meant a great deal. " Let us come over here and look out at the snow," she said at last, and they stood together in the deep window recess and looked out. The new snow was sparkling under the moon ; the park stretched away, dark woodland and open country, as far as one could see; off on the horizon were the twinkling lights of a large

town. Lady Mary did not say anything more,
but her arm was round Betty still, and presently Betty's head found its way to Lady
Mary's shoulder as if it belonged there. The
top of her young head was warm under Lady
Mary's cheek.

"Everybody is lonely sometimes, darling,"
said Lady Mary at last; "and as for me, I
am very lonely indeed, even with all my
friends, and all my cares and pleasures. The
only thing that really helps any of us is being
loved, and doing things for love's sake; it
is n't the things themselves, but the love that
is in them. That 's what makes Christmas so
much to all the world, dear child. But everybody misses somebody at Christmas time;
and there 's nothing like finding a gift of
new love and unlooked-for pleasure."

"Lady Dimdale helped us splendidly. It
would n't have been half so nice if it had n't
been for her," said Betty softly, — for her
Christmas project had come to so much more
than she had dreamed at first.

There was a stir in the drawing-room, and

a louder sound of voices. The gentlemen were coming in. Lady Mary must go back ; but when she kissed Betty again, there was a tear on her cheek, and so they stood waiting a minute longer, and loving to be together, and suddenly the sweet old bells in Danesly church, down the hill, rang out the Christmas chimes.

9 7 8 3 7 4 1 1 9 4 4 1 2